P9-CQA-372

Oh, Fudge!

Wishbone tried to stir the fudge, but the wooden spoon didn't budge. It was welded to a thick layer on the bottom of the pan that was as hard as cement. He tilted the kettle to one side and peered at the bottom. "We have reinvented coal," he said.

"Keep stirring," Peter said, as he opened some windows. "Maybe the top part will be OK."

Wishbone got a different spoon and stirred with it. "Little flecks of black cement keep coming loose," he said. "The fudge has freckles." He dipped a clean spoon into the fudge, blew on it, and popped the spoonful in his mouth.

"How's it taste?" Peter asked.

Wishbone grabbed a paper towel and spit out the fudge. "Like charcoal," he said. "We're doomed."

WITHDRAWN

Books by Peg Kehret

Available from MINSTREL Books

For orders other than by individual consumers, Pocket Books grants a discount on the purchase of **10 or more** copies of single titles for special markets or premium use. For further details, please write to the Vice-President of Special Markets, Pocket Books, 1633 Broadway, New York, NY 10019-6785, 8th Floor.

For information on how individual consumers can place orders, please write to Mail Order Department, Simon & Schuster Inc., 200 Old Tappan Road, Old Tappan, NJ 07675.

PB
FIC
KEH
4066

THE
RICHEST KIDS IN TOWN

PEG KEHRET

Library Media Center
Longwood Elementary School
30W240 Bruce Lane
Naperville, IL 60563

A MINSTREL® BOOK

Published by POCKET BOOKS
New York   London   Toronto   Sydney   Tokyo   Singapore

The sale of this book without its cover is unauthorized. If you purchased
this book without a cover, you should be aware that it was reported to
the publisher as "unsold and destroyed." Neither the author nor the publisher has received payment for the sale of this "stripped book."

This book is a work of fiction. Names, characters, places and incidents
are products of the author's imagination or are used fictitiously. Any
resemblance to actual events or locales or persons, living or dead, is
entirely coincidental.

A Minstrel Book published by
POCKET BOOKS, a division of Simon & Schuster Inc.
1230 Avenue of the Americas, New York, NY 10020

Copyright © 1994 by Peg Kehret

Reprinted by arrangement with Cobblehill Books, an affiliate of
Dutton Children's Books, a division of Penguin Books USA Inc.

All rights reserved, including the right to reproduce
this book or portions thereof in any form whatsoever.
For information address Cobblehill Books, an affiliate of
Dutton Children's Books, a division of Penguin Books USA Inc.,
375 Hudson Street, New York, NY 10014

ISBN: 0-671-52940-4

First Minstrel Books printing March 1997

10 9 8 7 6 5 4 3 2

A MINSTREL BOOK and colophon are registered trademarks of
Simon & Schuster Inc.

Cover art by Jean Francois Podevin

Printed in the U.S.A.

For my best friend,
CARL

Contents

Dear Tommy:

How is everything back home? I sure miss you. My new teacher is OK but I eat lunch alone every day. I'm saving my money so I can come to visit you next summer.

Your best friend forever,
Peter

1

Partners

Slam!

Peter gave his bedroom door an extra shove, after it was already closed, but he could still hear the laughter coming from his sister's room. Kathy and Sharon were at it again. Yakity, yakity, yak. Giggle, giggle, giggle. Nonstop nonsense.

Peter flopped face down on the bed and put the pillow over his head. He had thought a new town and a new school would be exciting. Now he knew they could be lonely, as well.

Where the Dodges used to live, Peter and his best friend, Tommy, had a secret joke. They would say the joke's key word in public and burst out laughing while everyone else wondered what was so funny.

Now Kathy was the only one laughing. She had

found Sharon right away; Peter still didn't have a friend.

Peter reached under his pillow and took out his blue money ideas notebook. Across the front in big red letters, it said: WAYS TO MAKE MONEY.

He opened the notebook and read the first page.

GOAL: *Earn $235 so I can go visit Tommy.*
Amount saved so far: $6.80

He planned to save every dime he made until he had $235, the cost of a round-trip plane ticket. He would spend a whole, wonderful week at Tommy's house, even if it took five years to earn enough money.

The trouble is, he thought, it might really take that long and who was he going to play with in the meantime?

He rolled over and stared at the ceiling, thinking about the kids he had met at his new school. Mark and Clinton were nice. So was Susie. Annabelle bragged too much; Peter avoided her like a finicky eater avoids Brussels sprouts.

And then there was Wishbone. Wishbone Wyoming.

Peter said the name out loud, the way a game show host might announce the next contestant. It was the best name he had ever heard.

His own name, Peter Dodge, was all right, except for being the same as his dad and his grandfather.

4

He was really Peter Dodge the Third, though he never wrote "III" after his name. He wished his parents had given him a name all his own. It got confusing when someone called and asked to speak to Peter. Of course, since he moved, no one called him anymore so it didn't matter what his name was. Probably no one would ever call him again.

Imagine being lucky enough to have Wyoming for a last name. Or any state, for that matter. Peter Arizona. Peter Wisconsin. Peter Montana. Now those were names that people would notice and remember. Anyone named Peter Arizona would be sure to get lots of phone calls.

It wasn't only Wishbone's name that Peter liked. It was his sense of humor. When Wishbone made up puns, even the teacher laughed.

Peter wished there was a Best Friend Store, where he could go to shop. At a Best Friend Store, you could walk up and down and look at all the kids in town and then select the person you most wanted for your best friend and he would instantly want you for a best friend, too. If Peter ever went to a Best Friend Store, he would choose Wishbone. Of course, Tommy would still be his out-of-town best friend. But it would be nice to have a friend like Wishbone, too, who went to the same school and lived nearby. Someone he could visit without earning $235 first.

Kathy's and Sharon's voices grew louder and

Peter realized they had left Kathy's room because Sharon was leaving. " 'Bye," Kathy said. "Call me tonight."

Peter wondered what they would have to say to each other tonight. They had been talking all afternoon. If Sharon had something to tell Kathy, there had been plenty of time.

Kathy tapped on Peter's door. "What are you doing?" she asked, after Peter told her to come in.

"Nothing."

"Want to play chess?" she asked.

Peter shook his head. He wasn't in the mood to play games, at least not with his sister. He wanted to play games with Tommy. His eyes filled with tears.

"What's the matter?" asked Kathy.

Peter looked away. "I miss Tommy." He braced himself for Kathy to say what his parents had said: it was easy to make new friends; all he had to do was be friendly to the kids in his new class and before he knew it he would forget all about Tommy.

Well, he didn't want to forget about Tommy. He wanted to move back to their old house and say the secret joke and have Tommy laugh with him.

Kathy said, "I don't blame you. It's tough to start a new school."

"You have Sharon."

"But I still get homesick sometimes for our old house, and for my old friends."

6

"I'm going to earn lots of money and buy a plane ticket and go visit Tommy."

Kathy considered that for a moment. Then she said, "In the meantime, while you're earning the money, you need to make some new friends here. You won't miss Tommy quite so much if you have a new friend."

Peter bit his bottom lip. "I'll never have friends here."

"Do an experiment," she said. "Every day during recess, talk to one person that you might like for a friend. See how long it takes before one of them talks to you first."

Peter was silent, thinking about her suggestion.

"You could start with the person you like best in your class. Just go up to him and say something."

"What should I say?"

"Ask him a question. Tell him you like his shirt and ask him where he got it. Or ask him what his favorite TV show is. If you ask a question, he'll answer and maybe you'll find something else to talk about."

Peter spent the rest of the time until dinner thinking up clever questions to ask for his experiment and deciding which one to use first. One thing he didn't have to decide was which kid to talk to. Kathy had said to start with the person he liked best. That would be Wishbone Wyoming.

The next day during recess, Peter approached Wishbone. "Is Wishbone your real name?" he asked.

"No. I hate my real name."

"What is it?"

"If I tell you, will you promise not to laugh?"

"Cross my heart."

"I am officially Winston Wyoming the Third."

"I'm a Third, too," Peter said. "Peter Dodge the Third."

"No kidding! I never knew another kid who was a Third. I think my parents should have been more original, instead of naming me the same as my dad and my grandpa."

"At least they gave you a good nickname."

"My grandpa doesn't think so. He always calls me Winston." Wishbone pointed at Peter and then at himself. "We can be a math problem," he said. "One boy plus one boy equals two-thirds."

Peter grinned. This conversation was going so well, he decided to ask the question he had planned to ask tomorrow. "If you had a hundred dollars," he said, "what would you buy?"

Before Wishbone could reply, Annabelle, who was standing nearby, butted in. "My father has tons of money," Annabelle said, as if that fact somehow made her special. "A hundred dollars is no big deal when you're as rich as I am."

Furious with her for interrupting, Peter blurted out, "*I'm* going to be rich, too."

"When?" said Annabelle.

"Before next summer."

"Sure you are," Annabelle said. "And I'll be playing quarterback for the Forty-niners."

"With your figure," said Wishbone, "you should play tackle."

Annabelle stomped indignantly away, while Peter and Wishbone chuckled.

"Are you really going to be rich?" asked Wishbone. "Or were you just trying to shut Annabelle up?"

"Both. I'm going to earn $235 before summer vacation." Peter had not intended to tell anyone about his plan to make money; it just slipped out when Annabelle started bragging.

"Why do you need so much money?" Wishbone asked.

"For a plane ticket. So I can visit my friend."

"I want to make money, too. There's a DC-3 model kit that I want to buy and it'll take me forever to save enough from my allowance."

"I have a notebook of WAYS TO MAKE MONEY. There are some terrific ideas."

"If they're so terrific, why aren't you rich already?"

"I need a partner." It was true, Peter decided. He had not known until that moment that he needed a partner but if Wishbone wanted to work with him, Peter was positive that his ideas would succeed. He'd probably have enough money to visit Tommy long before next summer.

"Could I help?" Wishbone asked.

"Sure. With two of us working, we'll make money twice as fast."

"That makes *cents*," said Wishbone.

Peter laughed. "We'll be the richest kids in town," he said.

"Good. Then Annabelle can quit boasting."

The bell rang, signaling the end of recess.

"Meet me after school," Peter said, "and we'll make money fast." He spent the rest of the day deciding which of his many brilliant ideas to use first.

At 3:15, when Mrs. Rather dismissed her fourth-grade class, most of the students exploded out the door. Wishbone and Peter lingered to make plans.

The boys discovered that they lived only three blocks apart and could walk partway home from school together.

"Do you have any pets?" Peter asked. "Do you know how to take care of animals?"

"I have a cat," said Wishbone. "Einstein. I take care of him."

"I have a dog," said Peter. "I take care of Scruffy all the time."

Peter held out his hand and Wishbone shook it. "We're partners," said Peter, "in The Scruffy-Einstein Pet Sitting Service, specializing in dogs and cats."

That afternoon, they wrote notices about their service and took them around their neighborhood.

"If people had pet deer," said Wishbone, "we could advertise that we'll do anything for a *buck*."

Peter hooted. Wishbone was going to be a fantastic business partner.

Dear Tommy:

Yesterday I was supposed to get
one dollar for pulling weeds but Mom
only paid me fifty cents because she
said I spent half my time playing
with Scruffy.
Another kid and I have started a
pet sitting service but so far we don't
have any customers. It is going to be
harder than I thought to earn
enough money for my plane ticket.

Your best friend,
Peter

2

The Scruffy-Einstein
Pet Sitting Service

On Saturday morning, while the Dodges were eating breakfast, the telephone rang. Kathy answered. Kathy always answered. Even if she was eating strawberry shortcake, or pepperoni pizza with extra cheese, Kathy leaped from her chair and rushed to the telephone. Peter knew she always answered because she hoped it would be Sharon. She was usually right.

This time, however, Kathy said, "Just a moment, please." She put her hand over the receiver and whispered, "Someone wants The Scruffy-Einstein Pet Sitting Service. They asked for Peter."

Peter jumped to his feet and grabbed the phone. A few minutes later, he called Wishbone. "Wash your face," he said. "We have a job interview in half an hour."

"Who's interviewing us?"

"Two dogs."

"That's a likely *tail*," said Wishbone.

Peter was too excited to appreciate the pun. "Someone named Rita Benson called. She knows your mom. She wants us to come to her house and meet her two dogs. If they like us, we get hired to come in every day after school and let the dogs out and play with them."

"What if they don't like us?"

"Of course they'll like us. Why wouldn't they like us?"

"What kind of dogs are they?" asked Wishbone.

"I didn't ask."

"I hope they aren't mean."

Half an hour later, the boys knocked on Rita Benson's door. Instantly, they heard loud barking from inside.

"They sound big," said Wishbone.

"Get your biscuit ready," said Peter. He had brought two of Scruffy's dog biscuits along, and had given one to Wishbone. "Dogs always like anyone who feeds them."

The door opened. Two giant schnauzers and a tiny woman greeted them. "Down, Queenie," said the woman. "Stay down. Down, King."

Peter held out his biscuit. Queenie swallowed it

whole. Wishbone tossed his biscuit on the floor. King crunched it quickly.

"How clever of you!" cried Rita. "The dogs love anyone who feeds them."

Queenie and King wagged their stubby tails, Peter and Wishbone petted them, and The Scruffy-Einstein Pet Sitting Service had its first regular client. Rita paid them five dollars in advance for the first week and gave them a key to her house.

"Way to go, Partner," Wishbone said, as soon as they were alone. "The biscuits did it."

"Let's take two dog biscuits with us every day so Queenie and King will always let us in."

"We can buy a box out of our first week's pay."

The dog biscuits were $1.98. They divided the rest of the money equally. Wishbone spent part of his on a bag of chocolate-covered peanuts but Peter mentally added $1.51 to the amount he had toward his plane ticket. They hurried home to see if any more customers had called.

On their first two days in business, The Scruffy-Einstein Pet Sitting Service threw balls for Queenie and King and played with a ropelike tug toy.

On the third day, Wishbone had a dentist appointment after school, so Peter went to Rita's house alone. He unlocked the door and gave the dogs their biscuits. Before he could take Queenie and King outside, someone rang the doorbell.

The dogs barked. Peter hesitated. He knew never to open the door to a stranger. At home, he was instructed to call out, asking who was there. Should he do that here, when it wasn't his house? Or should he pretend no one was home?

"Yoo-hoo," called the woman who rang the bell. "Little boy! I live next door to Rita and I want to use your pet sitting service, too."

Peter relaxed. Since the woman had obviously talked to Rita Benson about him, she wasn't the same as a stranger. Peter disliked being called "little boy," but it would be fun to surprise Wishbone with another customer.

He opened the door. Queenie and King bolted out.

"Queenie!" Peter yelled. "King! Come back."

"Little boy," said the woman who had knocked. "Rita's dogs are loose."

The dogs raced down the sidewalk. Peter dashed after them.

"There they go," said the woman.

"Queenie," called Peter. "Come get your biscuit." He held out his fists, pretending he had a dog biscuit in each hand. Queenie stopped. "Biscuit time," Peter said. "Yum, yum." King stopped.

Peter walked slowly toward them. "Come and eat your biscuit." Tails wagged. When he was close enough, he grabbed a collar in each hand and led the dogs toward home.

"I've changed my mind about hiring you," said the neighbor. "I can't gamble on someone who lets the dogs run loose; Fifi might go in the street." She went back to her own house.

Peter didn't answer. He was afraid if he said what he was thinking, the neighbor would be so shocked she would complain to Rita, and The Scruffy-Einstein Pet Sitting Service would get fired for being rude.

King and Queenie didn't want to go home. They wanted to sniff a tree.

"Biscuit," Peter said. "As soon as we get home, you get an extra treat." King and Queenie lurched ahead, with Peter's hands clinging to their collars.

He got them up the steps to Rita's front door. The door was closed. The neighbor must have shut it.

Peter let go of Queenie just long enough to grab the door knob. It didn't open.

Peter got a sick feeling inside. He tried again. Nothing happened.

The door was locked, and the key was lying inside on the kitchen counter, where he always put it while he and Wishbone played ball with Queenie and King.

He led the dogs around the side of the house. He opened the gate, and put the dogs in the fenced backyard where they would be safe. Peter tried the back door, just in case it was unlocked. It wasn't.

How was he going to get in the house? He didn't want to call Rita and confess he had left the key inside and locked himself out. She would probably say if The Scruffy-Einstein Pet Sitting Service was that stupid, she didn't need them anymore.

Peter jiggled all of the windows. None of them opened. He wondered if Queenie and King were angry because he had promised them an extra treat and failed to give it to them.

"I don't usually lie," he told them. "This was an emergency." Queenie and King dropped their balls at his feet, waiting for him to play.

Peter wondered if the next door neighbor might have a key to Rita's house. Neighbors sometimes do. Leaving the dogs in the yard, he went out the gate. He didn't want to talk to the woman who had caused all the trouble, but he couldn't think what else to do.

She did not have a key. "You'll need to call a locksmith," she said. "A locksmith can get the door open without damaging anything." She looked in the telephone directory and found a number for Peter; thirty minutes later, the locksmith was there with a bag of tools.

He got the door open easily and then handed Peter the bill. "That'll be $32.50," he said.

Peter gulped. "Can my mother send you a check?" he said.

"No credit," said the locksmith. "Sorry."

"But I don't have any money with me," said Peter. He did not add that at home he had a grand total of $8.31.

Wishbone arrived. "I had a cavity," he said. "My jaw is full of novocaine."

Peter told him what had happened.

Wishbone said, "I thought going to the dentist was the worst thing that would happen to me today but this is even worse. Where are we going to get $32.50?"

"Tell you what," said the locksmith. "I'll make an exception this one time. Sounds like you boys have had enough trouble for one day. Your mother can send the check to the address on the bill."

"Thanks," said Peter, as the locksmith left.

"Thirty-two dollars and fifty cents," moaned Wishbone. "We'll have to take care of Queenie and King for seven weeks before we break even."

"You don't have to pay half for the locksmith," said Peter. "You weren't even here."

"The same thing could have happened to me," Wishbone said. "Partners should stick together."

A warmth spread through Peter's insides, as if he had drunk a big mug of creamy rich hot chocolate. Instead of feeling angry at the neighbor and worried about the money, he felt glad to have such a loyal partner.

When he got home, Peter tied Rita's house key on a string, so he could wear it around his neck. He also set out six dog biscuits to take to Queenie and King, to make up for tricking them about the extra treats.

On Friday, when Peter and Wishbone arrived to play with Queenie and King, they found a note from Rita.

> *Dear Scruffy-Einstein Pet Sitting Service:*
> *I won't be needing you anymore after today.*
> *I have a new job in Toledo and will be moving this weekend. Thanks for your good service.*
> *Queenie and King will miss you.*

"We're unemployed," said Peter.

"And we're in debt," said Wishbone. "We owe your mom $32.50."

"We'll pay her out of the profits from our next customer."

"Do we have another customer?"

"No. Not yet."

"I'll pay my half out of my allowance," Wishbone said.

When Mrs. Dodge learned that The Scruffy-Einstein Pet Sitting Service had lost its only customer, she said the boys did not have to repay her for the locksmith.

Peter hugged his mother. Ordinarily, she would insist that he repay any money he borrowed. Peter suspected she knew how much he wanted Wishbone to be his friend. Maybe, by telling him and Wishbone they didn't have to pay back the money, his mom was trying to make it easier for the friendship to grow.

"Thanks, Mom," he said.

"The locked door really wasn't your fault," she said.

"It wasn't yours, either," said Wishbone.

"True," said Mrs. Dodge. "However, I have the $32.50, and you don't."

"All we have," said Peter, "is a box of dog biscuits."

Scruffy wagged his tail eagerly.

The boys took two apples out to the front steps.

"For our next money-maker," said Peter, "let's . . ."

"Not me," said Wishbone.

"But . . ."

"You can get rich by yourself."

Peter took a bite of his apple but he didn't chew it. He stared at the ground. Wishbone didn't want to be partners anymore. The Scruffy-Einstein Pet Sitting Service was a great big flop.

Dear Tommy:

Why don't you write? Are you OK? I thought I'd hear from you by now. There's nothing new here. My address is on the envelope, in case you lost it. Write soon.

Your best friend always,
Peter

3

The Great Duck Race

PRIVATE! KEEP OUT! NO PEEKING!
THIS MEANS YOU, KATHY.

Peter blew the dust off the warning clipped to the cover of his secret notebook. It was time to show the notebook to Wishbone. When Wishbone saw all of Peter's fine get-rich ideas, he wouldn't be able to resist being partners again.

Peter had not continued Kathy's experiment. He didn't want to talk to someone new each day. He wanted to talk to Wishbone.

Sometimes he did. Sometimes they even played together during recess. But they had not done anything together outside of school since their pet sitting partnership ended a week ago. Those few days when The Scruffy-Einstein Pet Sitting Service was in business were the most fun days since Peter had moved. Now, Peter decided, it was time to try again.

He dialed Wishbone's number. Ten minutes later, Wishbone sat on the side of Peter's bed. He had brought a bag of marshmallows with him. "What did you want to show me?" he asked. He tossed a marshmallow in the air and caught it in his mouth.

Peter held up the bright blue notebook.

Wishbone read out loud, "WAYS TO MAKE MONEY."

"This notebook," Peter said, "is full of clever ideas."

Wishbone threw another marshmallow in the air. This time he missed and Scruffy grabbed the marshmallow and swallowed it whole. "What clever ideas?" Wishbone asked.

"For starters, we're going to sponsor a duck race."

Wishbone ate a marshmallow without bothering to toss it in the air first. "How do you race ducks?" he said. "While they're flying? Swimming? Waddling?"

"Not *real* ducks. Plastic ducks. Like this." Peter opened his desk drawer and took out a bright yellow plastic duck. It had an orange beak and brown eyes.

"That's a baby toy. To use in the bathtub."

Peter turned the duck upside down. On the flat

bottom he had written a large number one. "We will buy fifty ducks," he said.

"Wait a minute. *I* am not buying fifty baby toys. I'm saving up to buy a model airplane kit at Shetland's Toy Store. It's a DC-3."

"You can buy the DC-3 kit with your profit from the duck race."

"I'm not sponsoring any duck race in a bathtub. You can *scrub* that idea."

Peter, ignoring the pun, shook his head sadly. "My own partner," he said, "doesn't give me credit for having a brain."

Wishbone chewed a marshmallow and waited.

"We'll buy fifty ducks," Peter continued, "and number each one on the bottom. We can get the ducks at the import store for only twenty cents each and then we'll sell them for two dollars and . . ."

"Hold it," Wishbone said. "Why would anyone pay us two dollars if they can buy a duck themselves for twenty cents?"

"We won't sell just a duck. We'll sell an entry in The Great Duck Race. Each duck will be numbered. We keep track of who buys what number. Like this."

He opened his notebook and showed Wishbone a page with the numbers one through fifty written down the left side. After #1, it said: Peter Dodge. After #2, it said: Wishbone Wyoming. "We each get a duck free, because we're the sponsors of the race."

"If we win, it will look suspicious. Like we rigged the race."

Peter grinned at him. Wishbone had said, "We." They were going to be partners again and this time, Peter was sure, nothing would go wrong.

"There's no way to cheat," Peter said. "The race will be in Turtle Creek. We'll drop all the ducks off the bridge at the same time and the first one to reach the culvert, where the creek goes under the road, is the winner."

Wishbone nodded. Turtle Creek was shallow but it flowed swiftly. He had dropped twigs and leaves off the bridge many times and watched until they disappeared into the culvert. The duck race would work.

"What's the prize?"

"A twenty-dollar gift certificate from Shetland's Toy Store. We can buy it after we sell the first ten ducks."

Wishbone did some fast arithmetic. Fifty ducks times $2 each would be $100. Minus $4, because he and Peter weren't paying for their ducks, left $96. Minus the cost of the toy store gift certificate left $76. Minus the cost of the ducks. He started to do 50×20 cents in his head but before he finished Peter spoke.

"Total investment is $30. Total income is $96. That leaves a profit of $66. You can buy your DC-3 kit and have money left over."

"Maybe we should sell refreshments," said Wishbone. "Cheese and *quackers*."

Peter groaned but secretly he admired the way Wishbone could think of puns.

They each paid half the cost of the ducks. Peter numbered them with his black marker.

The only hard part was selling entries in The Great Duck Race. Mark and Susie wanted to buy ducks but they had no money. Except for Annabelle, none of the kids at school had two dollars.

"Is this how you plan to get rich?" Annabelle said, as she paid for her duck. "What a joke."

"Maybe we could fill her duck with cement," said Wishbone.

Mrs. Rather, their teacher, bought one duck. Peter's father bought one and Wishbone's mother bought one. Kathy wouldn't buy a duck until Peter promised to do the dishes all weekend. Wishbone's grandparents bought two.

"We need publicity," Peter said. After school the next day, they took the bus to the office of the daily newspaper, *The Herald*, and asked to speak to a reporter about The Great Duck Race. Two days later, Peter and Wishbone had their picture in *The Herald*, holding their basket of plastic ducks. The headline said, "Young Entrepreneurs Sponsor Duck Race." They sold the remaining ducks that same day.

The race was held at noon on Saturday. Because of the newspaper article, about thirty people showed up to watch, including the photographer from *The Herald*.

Peter stood on the bridge, ready to turn the basket upside down and drop all the ducks into Turtle Creek.

Wishbone waited at the culvert, to grab the winning duck. He wore rubber boots and stood in the creek.

Kathy was across the road, at the other end of the culvert, with a big fishnet. She was supposed to catch as many ducks as she could so that when Peter and Wishbone did The Great Duck Race next year, they could use the ducks again and make an even bigger profit.

Wishbone's grandfather, who had a watch with a second hand, had agreed to count down for them.

"The Great Duck Race is about to begin," he announced. "Ten . . . Nine . . . Eight . . . Seven . . ."

Peter lifted the basket and held it over the railing. Wishbone crouched tensely, like the goalie in a hockey game, watching for the winning duck.

"Six . . . Five. . . . Four. . . ."

Peter tilted the basket slightly.

"Three. . . . Two . . . One . . . GO!!!"

Peter flipped the basket. Fifty yellow ducks dropped into the water. The people on the creekbank cheered.

The ducks swirled and swam. A few floated too close to the bank and got tangled in the rushes. Three bobbed lazily behind a big rock, as if unsure which way to get around it. Most of the ducks sailed quickly toward the culvert.

Wishbone was ready. As the first duck approached the culvert, he lunged for it. He lost his balance and sank down on one knee in Turtle Creek, but he didn't care. He caught the duck. He stood up and held the winning duck high over his head. The crowd cheered again.

Wishbone waded out of the creek. Peter and Wishbone's grandfather, who had the numbered list, met him halfway to the bridge. The onlookers clustered around, waiting to hear which number had won the race.

Wishbone decided to make the moment as dramatic as possible. "Ladieees and Gentlemen," he said, in a loud voice, "The Great Duck Race is over and the winning duck is Number . . ."

He flipped the duck over.

The bottom was blank.

He turned to Peter. "You forgot to number the winning duck," he whispered. "Now what do we do?"

"Yes?" someone yelled. "What's the winning number?"

Just then Kathy dripped across the road with her fishnet full of ducks. "I caught most of them," she said, "but there's a problem. All the numbers washed off."

Peter grabbed the fishnet.

Grandpa Wyoming looked at the bottoms of several ducks. "Boys," he said, "you didn't use a *waterproof* marker."

"You boneheads," said Kathy.

Wishbone groaned.

The crowd grumbled.

The newspaper photographer burst out laughing and snapped several pictures.

Annabelle screeched, "I demand my money back, or my father will sue you."

An article in *The Herald* the next day was headlined, "Duck Race Entrants Cry Fowl!"

"I couldn't have said it better myself," said Wishbone.

Mr. Shetland was nice about taking back the gift certificate and the DC-3 kit that Wishbone had bought with his share of the money.

"I was going to start the DC-3 this afternoon,"

Wishbone said sadly. "I never even opened the box."

It took two days to return the money to everyone who had purchased a duck.

"We still have thirty-eight ducks," Peter told Wishbone. "Next time, we'll use a waterproof marker."

"There isn't going to be any next time," Wishbone said. "Not for me."

Peter knew what Wishbone meant by that. He meant he didn't want to be partners anymore. Peter didn't blame him. Why should a smart, funny kid like Wishbone want to be partners with someone who did everything wrong?

Kathy was right, Peter thought. I *am* a bonehead. I'm a bonehead and I'll never make enough money to go visit Tommy. He'll forget who I am and I'll never have another best friend. I'll grow up and finish school and be a wrinkled, bald grandfather with a long, gray beard and I'll never, ever have another best friend.

Dear Tommy:

Thanks for your letter. The secret
fort that you and Jason are building
sounds neat.
~~I wish~~
~~If only~~
Maybe I can see it when I come
next summer.

Your best friend,
Peter

4

Soul Soothers

CHOCOLATE IS FOREVER

Wishbone finished painting the sign and laid it to dry beside the other signs.

WHEN IN DOUBT, PIG OUT

GIVE ME HOT FUDGE SUNDAES OR GIVE ME DEATH

"This had better work," Wishbone said, more to himself than to Peter.

Peter knew Wishbone was worried that Soul Soothers might be another shooting star idea—brilliant at first but quick to vanish.

Peter got the idea when Wishbone hobbled in the door and eased himself into a chair, complaining about his father's health club. "Working out at Dad's club," Wishbone had said, as he ripped open a package of Oreo cookies, "is torture."

"It builds up your muscles."

"It builds up my appetite." He tried to eat the top half of the Oreo without getting any of the filling. "Dad says if it hurts, he knows his body is improving." He moved his head slowly from side to side, as if testing to see if it would stay on. "I wish he didn't want to improve *my* body."

Peter looked at Wishbone's pudgy middle and moon-shaped face. Wishbone would make a perfect "Before" picture for a diet ad. Peter could understand Mr. Wyoming's concern but he didn't say so. Instead, he picked up his blue notebook and began to write.

"Forget it," Wishbone said. "I'm too tired to get rich."

"This is a lucky idea because you're a Third and I'm a Third and this is our third idea. Haven't you heard that *the third time's the charm*?"

"No, but I've heard, *three strikes and you're out*."

"This idea will make us wealthy while we sit around and eat brownies."

Wishbone swallowed the top of the Oreo and began to lick the filling. "Explain," he said.

"I'll bet there are lots of people like you who hate working out. What they really want is a club where they can eat and be lazy. We are going to give them what they want—and make a profit."

Although the boys had played together several times since the duck race, Peter had held off suggesting another scheme to make money. But he did want to repay Wishbone for what he had lost on the duck race, and this new idea was foolproof.

Peter said, "We are now the co-owners of Soul Soothers." He was careful not to use the word *partners*. He didn't want to make Wishbone nervous.

"Soul Soothers?" said Wishbone. "It sounds like a church."

"It's a club that soothes the soul. With food."

"It isn't fair to do this when I'm not of sound body," complained Wishbone. But he shook Peter's hand, just the same.

Two hours later, as Wishbone finished the signs, Peter got up from his desk, and handed Wishbone a piece of paper. "The flyer is written," he said.

Wishbone read it.

Are you tired of treadmills? Sick of stair climbing? Bored with bicycles that go nowhere? Give your weary muscles a break. Try Soul Soothers. You'll have no goals to strive for, no charts to embarrass you, and no trainer urging you to work harder. What *you WILL have (for a tiny $3 fee) is rest, relaxation, and your choice of buttered popcorn, brownies, or hot fudge sundaes.*

SOUL SOOTHERS is the only club that satisfies your sweet tooth.

SOUL SOOTHERS Open daily, 4:00 - 5:30 PM

Wishbone let his breath out in a low whistle. "If there is a prize for best advertising flyer, you will win it," he said. "I'll ask my dad if we can make copies on his copy machine."

By the next day, they were ready. It had cost them $7.83 each for brownie mix, ice cream, fudge sauce, and popcorn. They didn't mind; the Soul Soother fees would soon pay them back.

"We only need five customers to meet our expenses," Peter said. "From then on, it will be pure profit."

"DC-3 kit," said Wishbone, "here I come."

They left for school two hours early and nailed forty flyers on telephone poles. At school, they taped another sixty flyers on lockers.

"Everyone's on a diet," Annabelle said, when she saw them taping up flyers. "Nobody wants to eat desserts."

After school, they rushed to Peter's house and baked five boxes of brownie mix. While the brownies were in the oven, they popped four big bowls of popcorn.

"After today," Peter said, "we'll know how much food to prepare. This first time, it's better to have too much than to chance running out." He took a bag of gingersnaps out of the cupboard, in case they needed them.

Wishbone heated the hot fudge sauce while Peter hung the signs in the living room. Then, to be sure the fudge sauce tasted good, they each had a sundae.

"This club," said Wishbone, "is a *sweet* idea."

While they waited for their customers to arrive, they nibbled on warm brownies. When nobody had come by 4:30, Peter began to pace back and forth in front of the window. Each time he passed the coffee table, he absentmindedly picked up another brownie.

Wishbone preferred to soothe his soul with gingersnaps and popcorn. He took a bite of cookie and then a handful of popcorn, followed by another bite of cookie. Scruffy sat on the floor beside him. Every few seconds, Wishbone tossed Scruffy some popcorn and Scruffy tried to catch it in the air. Twice Wishbone forgot which hand to use and threw Scruffy a gingersnap by mistake. Scruffy didn't mind. He just wagged his tail and drooled for more.

"Do you know anyone who's on a diet?" Peter asked.

"Only my mother."

"Maybe three dollars is too high," Peter said. "Maybe tomorrow we should lower the price. At two dollars, we'd still make a profit after eight customers."

Wishbone swallowed more popcorn. So did Scruffy.

"It must be the rain," Peter said. "People don't like to go out when it's raining."

Wishbone ate another gingersnap. So did Scruffy.

Peter's mother got home at 5:30. She looked at the signs. She looked at the empty brownie pan and the empty gingersnap bag and the two empty popcorn bowls. "I hope you don't get sick," she said.

"The food was for Soul Soothers," Peter said, "only no one came."

"It's a new club," Wishbone added.

Mrs. Dodge carried the empty brownie pan into the kitchen.

Peter sank down on the sofa beside Wishbone. "I liked my flyer," he said sadly. "I thought people would line up to get in."

"So did I."

Kathy came home from basketball practice. Sharon was with her. "Yum. I smell popcorn," Kathy said.

"Hold it," Peter said. "The goodies are only for

44

members of Soul Soothers. Membership fee is three dollars."

"Are *you* the ones who put those flyers all over town?" Sharon said.

Peter nodded.

"You blew it," Kathy said.

"What do you mean?"

"Some guys came in the school gym during basketball practice and asked if anyone knew where the Soul Soothers club was. Next time you print a flyer, put your address on it."

Wishbone grabbed the flyer and read it. Then he lay back on the sofa and groaned. "I don't feel so good," he said.

"Me, either," said Peter.

"Dinner in twenty minutes," Mrs. Dodge called.

Scruffy threw up.

While Peter scrubbed the carpet, he explained Soul Soothers to his mother.

"I'm glad you forgot the address," she said. "You can't invite complete strangers to come here and eat. Absolutely not."

"Our get-rich plans have put me in the hole," Wishbone said. "I'll never have that DC-3."

Peter noticed that Wishbone had said *our* plans, when he could have said, *your* plans. That's one thing Peter liked about Wishbone—no matter what went wrong, he never tried to blame it all on Peter.

"I'm sorry about the flyer," Peter said.

Wishbone said, "I read it, too, before we copied it, and I didn't notice that the address was missing."

Mrs. Dodge said, "There are four more pans of brownies in the kitchen. What are you going to do with them?"

"Eat them," said Wishbone.

"You've both had far too many sweets already."

"We could sell brownies at school tomorrow," Peter said.

"No, you couldn't," said Mrs. Dodge.

"You could give them to The Kettle Kitchen," said Sharon.

"Who?" said Peter.

"It's a group of volunteers who serve free meals to homeless people. Usually they just have soup and bread; brownies might be a treat."

"Who pays for the soup and bread?" Wishbone asked. "How can they give it away?"

"Lots of people help," Sharon said. "Civic groups and churches donate money or food. Last Thanksgiving, Mom and Dad gave them a turkey."

Wishbone gazed longingly at the rich, chocolate brownies.

"I went along," Sharon said, "when Mom and Dad took the turkey. If The Kettle Kitchen wasn't there, lots of people would go hungry. I'll bet some of them have never had a brownie."

Wishbone tried to imagine life without brownies. It was too horrible to think about.

Peter wondered how it would feel to have no dinner. Even though he wasn't hungry at the moment, he knew it would be terrible not to have food.

The two boys looked at each other and nodded. "Let's do it," they said, at exactly the same time.

"Maybe we can deliver the brownies tonight," Peter said, "while they're still fresh."

Wishbone agreed. "That way, I won't be tempted to eat them."

After Peter and Wishbone carefully packed all the brownies in boxes, Mr. Dodge drove the boys downtown. Clutching the boxes of brownies, they dashed through the rain from the car to The Kettle Kitchen.

A line of weary-looking people straggled out The Kettle Kitchen door. Inside, six men and women ladled steaming soup into bowls and passed baskets of bread to rows of people who slumped silently over chipped tables. The smell of onions and damp clothing tried unsuccessfully to mix.

Sharon was right, Peter thought. Some of these people would have no food if they didn't come here. He wondered what went wrong in people's lives so that they were unable to take care of themselves.

The boys handed their boxes to one of the servers.

"What group donated these?" she asked.

"Soul Soothers," said Peter.

"Who?" said Mr. Dodge.

The woman thanked them and then opened the first box and walked beside the tables, passing brownies to the diners.

Peter watched as a wrinkled old man, wearing a tattered overcoat and a red baseball cap, took a bite of brownie. The man chewed for a moment and then said, "This takes me back to my boyhood."

Peter felt Wishbone's hand slip into his and give it a squeeze.

After the man ate the rest of the brownie, he turned to look at Peter and Wishbone. He stood up, bowed slightly, and tipped his cap to them. "Thank you," he said.

"You're welcome," Peter said. He spoke quietly, as if he were in church. Beside him, Wishbone smiled silently at the old man.

The man sat back down and continued to eat his soup.

They didn't talk on the way home. Peter didn't feel like chattering; he needed to think about the people at The Kettle Kitchen and about how he felt when the old man thanked them for the brownies.

When Mr. Dodge stopped the car at Wishbone's house, Wishbone said, "Even though we didn't make any money, Soul Soothers turned out OK. That old man really liked his brownie."

Peter nodded. "Maybe we could take brownies there again some time."

"Yes," said Wishbone. "I'd like that."

The next morning, Annabelle saw the boys taking down their flyers. "I knew it," she said. "You didn't get rich; you didn't make any money, at all. Soul Soothers was a disaster."

"Soul Soothers," said Wishbone, "was a huge success. I'll never forget it."

"Oh," said Annabelle. She sounded disappointed.

Dear Tommy:

Is there any chance you could come here this summer, instead of me going there? I'm not sure I'll have the $235 in time.
Let me know right away.

Peter Dodge, III

P.S. I met a kid named Wishbone who is also the Third. We have decided it sounds distinguished.

5

The Three-Legged Race

"My little cousin is coming to visit," Wishbone said glumly. "He's four years old and follows me like a shadow."

Peter tried to look sympathetic but he was too excited about his good news to be upset over Wishbone's cousin. "I've found a way for us to make some money," he said.

"He still wets the bed," Wishbone said. He unwrapped an orange sour ball and popped it in his mouth.

"We're going to enter a three-legged race," Peter said. He pointed to a notice in the newspaper. "The Rotary Club is sponsoring Family Fun Day next Saturday, with contests and prizes. The prize for the three-legged race is ten dollars."

Wishbone looked at the notice. "There's a two-dollar entry fee," he said. "What if we don't win? We can't afford to lose a two-dollar entry fee."

"Read the whole thing. The only way we lose the entry fee is if we don't finish the race. Every team that finishes, no matter how slow, is guaranteed a two-dollar prize. Second place gets five dollars and the winners get ten dollars."

"My cousin's name is Boris and he carries a stuffed rabbit everywhere he goes," Wishbone said. "He's staying a whole week."

Peter put the newspaper down. It was unlike Wishbone to be so forlorn. Usually, Peter could count on Wishbone to make him laugh. "When is your cousin coming?" he asked.

"Tomorrow."

"If we enter the three-legged race, we'll need to practice a lot while Boris is here. You won't be home much."

Wishbone reached for a green sour ball. "That's right," he said. "We will need to practice every day. Maybe even twice a day. How do we enter?"

"At Kashner's Drug Store."

They took their two dollars to Kashner's and filled out an entry form.

"Let's start practicing," Peter said. "There's some clothesline rope in our garage."

They wound the rope around Peter's left leg and

Wishbone's right leg so that the two legs were held tightly together.

"This race won't have a winner," said Wishbone. "It will be a *tie*."

"Let's try to walk," said Peter.

It was trickier than they expected. Peter tended to move faster than Wishbone; the legs that were tied together felt like lead pipes. Twice the boys fell down.

"I feel like a domino," Wishbone said. "If you go down, I go, too."

"We need to count, like the military people do when they march," Peter said.

"Left and right won't work."

"We'll use In and Out. In means the inside legs that are tied together. Out means the outside legs."

Wishbone nodded.

"Out," Peter said. He and Wishbone both stepped forward with their free leg.

"In," Peter said. Together, they moved the two legs that were tied.

"Out. In. Out. In."

After they settled into the rhythm, they thumped all the way around the Dodge's yard without stumbling. Scruffy galloped in circles beside them, giving excited yips.

"We'll go a little faster every day," Wishbone said, "until we're running."

The next afternoon, Peter took his rope to Wishbone's house to practice. He found Wishbone on the floor, playing "Go Fish" with Boris.

"I've come to rescue you," Peter said.

As they walked outside, Wishbone whispered, "He wet his pants on the airplane. Mom says he got too excited." Wishbone wrinkled his nose. "He came off the plane in front of all those people with a big wet stain on his front."

Boris watched while Peter and Wishbone tied their legs together. When they chanted, "In, out, in, out," and marched up and down the sidewalk, Boris tagged after them, saying, "In, out," at the same time.

"I want to be in the race, too," Boris said.

"You can't," Wishbone said. "You don't have anyone to race with."

"I'm your cousin," Boris said. "You should race with me."

"Why don't you race with your rabbit?" Peter suggested.

"OK," Boris said.

Peter gave him some rope and helped him tie the rabbit to his leg. Then Peter and Wishbone practiced some more while Boris and Bunny trailed behind them, echoing their words.

"He'll be here six more days," Wishbone muttered. "I'm not sure I can stand it."

They practiced every day. When Wishbone went to Peter's house, Boris went, too, and took his rabbit. When they weren't practicing for the three-legged race, they played catch and taught Boris how to fly paper airplanes.

"Only three more days," said Wishbone. "If you weren't here to help me, I don't think I'd make it."

"He isn't such a bad kid," Peter said.

Friday night, they practiced their three-legged running for two hours. "We are good," Peter declared. "REALLY GOOD. I'll bet the second place runners don't even come close to us."

"Even if we don't win, it's been fun practicing. It made my week with Boris go a lot faster."

Family Fun Day started at ten o'clock Saturday morning. The three-legged race was the second event.

Peter knocked on Wishbone's door at eight, with the rope draped over his shoulder and a lucky penny in his pocket. His good running shoes were tied in double knots, to be sure he didn't trip.

Boris answered the door. "Wishbone has the chicken pox," he said. "There are little red bumps all over his stomach."

Peter stepped inside. He knew all about chicken pox; he had it when he was six. Wishbone lay on the sofa with a thermometer in his mouth. Mrs. Wyoming stood beside him, looking at her watch.

"Tell me it isn't true," Peter said.

"I'm sorry, Peter," Mrs. Wyoming said. "Wishbone won't be able to do the three-legged race with you."

Wishbone took the thermometer out of his mouth. "I'll put makeup on the spots," he said. "Nobody will know."

"You cannot expose all those people to the chicken pox," Mrs. Wyoming said. She turned to Peter. "Maybe your sister could do the race with you," she suggested.

Peter shook his head. "Kathy isn't home. She went somewhere with Sharon."

"I'll race with you, Peter," Boris said. "I know how."

Peter looked at Boris. He wore pink drop-seat pajamas with feet in them and clutched Bunny under one arm. Peter couldn't race in front of half the town with a baby for a partner.

"We'll forfeit the entry fee if we don't show up," Wishbone said.

"In, out, in, out," said Boris, as he marched around the room.

There were red bumps on Wishbone's face; he kept rubbing his temples, as if he had a headache.

"Don't scratch," Mrs. Wyoming said. "You'll get scars if you scratch."

Peter's mother had said exactly the same thing. It made Peter remember how awful he had felt when he had chicken pox. He wouldn't trade places with Wishbone for anything.

"Another two dollars down the drain," said Wishbone. "Just when I really believed we had a chance to win." He sounded like he was going to cry.

"In," said Boris. "Out. In. Out."

Peter thought how excited Wishbone would be if Peter and Boris won the three-legged race. If they won first place, Wishbone might even forget how much he itched. Even if they didn't win, he owed it to Wishbone not to forfeit the entry fee.

"Get dressed," Peter told Boris. "We have to be there by ten."

Boris dashed for the bedroom.

"The rabbit stays home," Peter yelled after him. There were limits to what he would do in public, even for Wishbone.

Family Fun Day attracted a large crowd. The Rotarians gave free balloons to children under six and the popcorn wagon did a brisk business.

There were ten other couples in the three-legged race. Peter tied his left leg and Boris's right leg together. "In, out," he said as they tried walking together. Boris's legs were much shorter than Wishbone's, so Peter had to remember to take smaller steps, but it wasn't as bad as Peter had feared. Boris's practice with Bunny had prepared him well.

They took their place at the starting line with the other contestants. Spectators lined both sides of the race area. Peter saw Mark and Annabelle in the front row. Mark waved and hollered, "Go, Peter!"

"This is the best thing I ever did in my whole life," Boris said. "I bet we'll win."

Win or lose, thought Peter, we'll have something interesting to tell Wishbone.

"On your mark," cried the announcer. "Get set. Go!"

"Out," yelled Peter.

"In," cried Boris.

"Out. In. Out! In!"

At the halfway mark, they were in second place. Peter chanted faster. "Out! In!! Out!! In!!"

They moved closer to the pair in front.

"OUT!!" Peter yelled. "IN!!"

"We're going to win!" screamed Boris.

And then Peter felt it. Something warm and wet was oozing across his left pant leg.

He looked down. A large stain covered the front of Boris's shorts. It was spreading rapidly across Peter's jeans.

60

Peter stopped running.

"Come on! We can win!" Boris cried.

Peter doubled over, trying to hide his pants.

"Are you all right?" someone asked. "Do you have a pain in your side?"

"I'm OK," Peter muttered.

Walking bent over, dragging a wailing Boris behind him, he hurried through the crowd. He heard the people cheer as the three-legged race ended. He heard the announcer declare the winners.

When they reached the edge of the park, Peter untied their legs. Even the rope was soaked. He wished he could go straight home and never see Boris again but he knew he had to take Boris back to Wishbone's house. Much as he would like to, he couldn't abandon Boris at the park.

Mrs. Wyoming gave Peter a pair of Wishbone's pants to wear home. They were too big but he wore them anyway.

"This only happens when he gets overexcited," Mrs. Wyoming said.

"What about our entry fee?" Wishbone asked. "Did you finish the race?"

Peter shook his head. "This," he said, "is the most disgusting thing that's ever happened to me."

"You forfeited," said Wishbone. "We've lost another two dollars."

"There were six zillion people watching that race. How could I finish in wet pants?"

Wishbone was quiet for a moment. Then he started to laugh.

"My sock was so wet," said Peter, "that I left it in a trash can."

Wishbone pointed at Peter's bare ankle and laughed harder.

"Mark and Annabelle were in the front row," Peter added. "Can you imagine what Annabelle would say if she had seen me racing with wet pants?"

Wishbone slapped his thigh in glee.

"I had to walk away doubled over."

Peter had hoped his report of the three-legged race would make Wishbone feel better; it certainly seemed to be working. The harder Wishbone laughed, the more details Peter told him.

At last Wishbone gasped, "It was worth two dollars to hear what happened."

"Thank you for letting Boris race with you," Mrs. Wyoming said. "It was very nice of you."

"Yes, it was," Wishbone said, suddenly serious. "Thanks, Peter the Third."

"You would have done the same for me," Peter said.

"Not with Boris, I wouldn't. That kid . . ." he hesitated a second and then finished, "is all wet."

Boris reappeared, wearing clean clothes.

"I'm going home," said Peter.

"Can I go with you?" asked Boris.

Wishbone guffawed.

"Good-bye, forever," said Peter, but he was laughing, too. Despite losing the entry fee and despite his embarrassment over his wet pants, the three-legged race had been worth the effort. Wishbone definitely felt better.

Dear Tommy:

I got your letter saying you are
going to camp with Jason this summer and can't come here, too. Sorry it
took me so long to write back. I've
been really busy.

Remember that kid I told you
about—Wishbone? Well, he and I
built crutches out of some scrap wood
in his grandpa's garage. We told this
dumb girl named Annabelle that we
have a contagious disease that makes
our legs weak. Maybe now she will
leave us alone.

We're going to make Valentine
baskets and fill them with homemade
fudge and sell them.

                              Your friend,
                              Peter

6

Candy Corn Valentines

"Our valentine baskets," said Peter, "will be a sensation."

"So was the duck race," said Wishbone. "Maybe we should shoot baskets instead, or ride our bikes to the park."

"You'll need to taste the fudge a lot," said Peter, "to be sure it's good."

"That," said Wishbone, "is known as bribery."

They found a recipe in one of Mrs. Dodge's cookbooks and followed it carefully. Wishbone stirred the fudge, tasting it often, while Peter drew hearts and tulips on a red paper basket.

When the fudge was cold, they cut it into thirty-two squares and put eight pieces in the red basket.

They planned to show the basket to people and take orders.

"We can use the rest of this fudge for the first three baskets we sell," Peter said.

Wishbone looked wistfully at the pan of fudge. He licked his lips. "Valentine's Day is four days away," he said. "We will need fresh fudge, not dried out four-day-old fudge." He reached for the pan.

"We'll freeze it," Peter said. He wrapped the fudge in foil and put it in the freezer.

Seven people said they might buy baskets but only two of them were willing to pay in advance.

Peter was undaunted. "When Valentine's Day arrives," he said, "people will buy our baskets. I'm sure of it."

Wishbone hoped he was right. Peter did have good ideas and most of the time it wasn't his fault that they didn't work.

On February 13th, Peter and Wishbone bought ten pounds of sugar, two boxes of baking chocolate, two pounds of butter and a half-gallon of milk. Even with a coupon for twenty-five cents off on the butter, it took all the money they had received for the two prepaid baskets, plus Peter's allowance, plus two dollars that Wishbone's uncle gave Wishbone when he came to pick up Boris.

They got out Mrs. Dodge's big stainless steel kettle, the one she uses to make strawberry jam every summer. They tripled the fudge recipe that they had used before, carefully measuring all of the ingredients.

The fudge burbled to a boil while Peter stirred with the biggest wooden spoon he could find. Wishbone buttered three square pans and set them side by side, ready to receive the finished fudge.

"YIIIIPE!" The loud, shrill bark made both boys jump.

"That sounds like Scruffy," Peter said. He stopped stirring and ran to the front door.

"YIPE! YIP YIP YIP YIIIPE!!"

"It *is* Scruffy. HELP! A big dog is killing Scruffy." Peter rushed to the kitchen and grabbed a broom. "Come on!" he yelled.

Wishbone raced after Peter.

Snarls, yips, and growls blended together as the two dogs nipped and snapped at each other. Peter raised the broom over his head but Scruffy and the big dog were circling so fast that Scruffy's black fur and the other dog's white fur swirled together like a spinning top. Peter was afraid if he whacked at the big dog he would hit Scruffy by mistake.

Wishbone snatched the Dodge's garden hose. He turned on the faucet and aimed the hose at the two dogs. When the cold water hit them, they leaped apart. Peter grabbed Scruffy. The big white dog shook his fur indignantly and then galloped down the street.

Peter carried a drenched, whimpering Scruffy inside. The two boys checked him carefully but despite his sad eyes and whining, he seemed uninjured.

"It's your own fault," Peter told him, "for digging under the fence. Why can't you stay in the backyard, where you belong?" But even though Peter sounded cross, he kept hugging Scruffy and Wishbone knew Peter was glad that Scruffy was safe.

Peter got a towel from the bathroom and blotted Scruffy's fur. They sat on the floor with Scruffy between them and petted him. Scruffy thumped his tail on the floor.

"What's that funny smell?" Wishbone said. "Did Scruffy roll in your compost pile again?"

A shrill, sharp sound came from the kitchen. *Bleep. Bleep. Bleep.*

"The smoke alarm," Peter said.

"Our fudge!" Wishbone cried.

Black fudge bubbled over the top of the kettle. Like volcanic lava, it flowed down the sides and onto the hot burner. Dark smoke rose toward the ceiling.

Bleep. Bleep. Bleep.

Peter turned off the stove. He grabbed a pot holder and pulled the kettle off the burner.

"Keep stirring," he said, "while I disconnect the smoke alarm."

Wishbone tried to stir the fudge but the wooden spoon didn't budge. It was welded to a thick layer on the bottom of the pan that was hard as cement. He tilted the kettle to one side and peered at the bottom. "We have reinvented coal," he said.

"Keep stirring," Peter said, as he opened some windows. "Maybe the top part will be OK."

Wishbone got a different spoon and stirred with it. "Little flecks of black cement keep coming loose," he said. "The fudge has freckles." He dipped a clean spoon into the fudge, blew on it, and popped the spoonful into his mouth.

"How's it taste?" Peter asked.

Wishbone grabbed a paper towel and spit out the fudge. "Like charcoal," he said.

"It can't be that bad."

"You taste it."

Peter took a spoonful. He managed to swallow it but he knew there was no way they could use it in their valentine baskets. He poured himself a glass of milk and drank it, to get the taste of the fudge out of his mouth.

"We're doomed," Wishbone said.

"We still have the baskets."

"Empty baskets."

"We'll make more candy."

"How? We used all the sugar. And all the butter and all the chocolate." Wishbone slumped against the kitchen counter. "And all our money."

"I'll think of something," said Peter.

"You'd better think fast. Unless you have a bunch of candy hidden away somewhere, there's no way we can . . ."

"That's it! We'll use my Halloween candy. I never ate it."

"You didn't eat your Halloween candy?" Wishbone's astonishment made his voice squeak.

"I caught a cold on Halloween night and didn't have any appetite for a few days and then I forgot about it."

"You *forgot* your Halloween candy?" Wishbone knew he sounded stupid, repeating everything Peter said, but he couldn't help himself. How could anyone forget about Halloween candy? Never in a trillion zillion years would Wishbone still have trick-or-treat candy left in February. His was always gone by November second. Sometimes even November first.

Peter went into his bedroom and rummaged around in the closet. "Bingo!" he yelled.

He emerged with a crumpled orange and black bag filled with assorted treats.

"We promised homemade fudge," Wishbone said, "not stale candy corn."

72

"Everything is wrapped, so it's still good. And no one will know it's Halloween candy. We'll melt it all together and then let it get hard and cut it in squares, like fudge."

They tried to scrape the black cement out of the kettle but it wouldn't come loose. "We can do this later," Peter said. "Let's use a different pan."

They began unwrapping the trick-or-treat candy and tossing it into Mrs. Dodge's electric frying pan. "Set the heat on low," Peter said. "We don't want it to burn."

Wishbone unwrapped two Snickers bars and put them in the frying pan. Then he dumped in a package of Milk Duds.

Peter added three black licorice sticks and some malted milk balls.

Wishbone gave it all a stir. He opened two packages of orange pumpkins and witches and poured them in. Peter broke up two Hershey bars and sprinkled the pieces on top.

"Oh, boy," Wishbone said, as he reached into the bag. "You have some Reese's Peanut Butter Cups. They're my favorite."

"In the pan," Peter said, pointing. "No eating."

"Just one?"

"We may not have enough."

Reluctantly, Wishbone plucked the individual Reese's cups out of their paper holders and added them to the mixture in the frying pan. The various chocolates began to melt, and so did the pumpkins and witches.

While Wishbone stirred, Peter added the rest of the trick-or-treat goodies: two boxes of Junior Mints, four pieces of bubble gum, a sack of salted peanuts, three bags of candy corn, a Milky Way, and a box of raisins.

"It doesn't look very appetizing," Wishbone said.

"It will when it blends together."

"I don't think the licorice is going to melt."

Kathy came sniffing into the kitchen. She looked at the blackened kettle and the mess where the fudge had boiled over on the stove. "Mom," she said cheerfully, "is going to kill you." She peered at the mixture in the frying pan and then covered her mouth and made gagging sounds.

"You don't have to eat it," Peter said.

"It's for our valentine baskets," Wishbone added.

Kathy rolled her eyes. "You'd better put some Mr. Yuk stickers on your baskets," she said. "That stuff would corrode the stomach of a robot."

The licorice didn't melt; Wishbone finally fished it out with a fork and ate it. When everything else was mixed together, more or less, they poured the contents of the frying pan into two of the buttered pans.

"It's awfully lumpy," Wishbone said.

"It has character," replied Peter. "These will be one-of-a-kind valentine baskets."

They went in Peter's room to play a game while they waited for the candy to harden.

While they were still deciding what to play, there was a scream from the kitchen.

"Your mother's home," said Wishbone.

"Oops," said Peter. "We forgot to clean up the stove."

Mrs. Dodge agreed that it was more important to save Scruffy's life than to stir the fudge. "But you could have started a fire," she said. "Always turn off the stove before you leave the kitchen."

She picked up her large kettle and carried it to the sink. Peter could tell by the way she moved that she was angry. His parents had always tried not to yell at him in front of his friends, no matter what kind of mischief he got into, but he had a feeling that this day was going to be an exception.

Mrs. Dodge took a deep breath and let it out slowly. She turned around, leaning her back against the sink. "When I get home from the hospital," she said, "I'm tired. I've been on my feet for eight hours, trying to help sick people get well."

Peter looked at the floor and said nothing.

"Do you know how I felt when I saw this mess?" Mrs. Dodge continued. "I wanted to cry."

"I'm sorry," said Peter. He felt like crying himself.

"I'm sorry, too," said Wishbone. "We're a couple of rats." He hoped Peter's mother didn't say Wishbone couldn't come over anymore. Even worse, what if she said Peter couldn't play with Wishbone at all?

To the boys' surprise, Mrs. Dodge smiled at them. "You aren't rats," she said. "You're two nice boys who made a mistake."

Peter scrubbed the stove while Wishbone, using a pick, chipped pieces of coal out of the big kettle. When he had most of it out, Mrs. Dodge filled the kettle with hot soapy water and said she would let it soak overnight.

By then, the recycled candy had hardened. They cut it in pieces and each boy ate one.

"What do you think?" Peter said.

"I think I should have eaten the Reese's Peanut Butter Cups. We wasted all that perfectly good candy."

Peter hated to admit it but the candy was awful. How could so many good flavors taste so terrible when they were mixed together?

"We'll have to give a refund to the people who prepaid," Peter said, as they scraped the concoction into the garbage can.

"We can't," Wishbone said. "We spent their money on the fudge ingredients."

"If you wanted candy," Mrs. Dodge said, "why didn't you eat that fudge you put in the freezer?"

"We're saved!" Peter said. "There's enough for the people who paid plus one more."

They removed the fudge from the freezer and divided the pieces among the three baskets.

Peter scribbled some figures on a scrap of paper. "After we sell the third basket," he said, "we'll still have $2.37 less than we started with."

"I don't think we should sell it," Wishbone said.

"We can't afford to eat it ourselves."

"I think we should give it to your mom."

Peter blinked in surprise. "You do?"

Wishbone continued. "How many moms would help us clean up such a mess without yelling the whole time?"

"Not many," Peter said. "She could have sent you home and told you never to come back."

"Or grounded you for a month. Or called my mom to say that I'm always getting you in trouble."

"*I'm* the one who gets us in trouble," Peter said. "If it weren't for me trying to earn money for my plane ticket, you'd have your DC-3 kit by now."

"I also would have missed the taste treat of the century: hot licorice dripping with melted bubble gum." He started to laugh. "It's the first time I ever had to hold my nose in order to eat candy."

Peter laughed, too.

Secretly, Wishbone wished Peter wouldn't go visit Tommy next summer. Despite all Peter's failed schemes, it would be awfully dull without him for a whole week. There would be no one to ride bikes with or play Nintendo with or go to the library with. Wishbone didn't like to think about it. But he knew Peter wanted to go, so Wishbone didn't say anything about wanting him to stay. He just hoped one of Peter's ideas would make a lot of money so Peter could afford the ticket.

"Let's make a valentine card," Wishbone said, "to go with your mom's basket of fudge."

Peter drew hearts and smiling faces on the front of the card while Wishbone wrote a poem for the inside:

> *"Your pan was black*
> *And we were blue*
> *You didn't yell,*
> *So we love you."*

They put the valentine basket and card on Mrs. Dodge's pillow and then shut the bedroom door so Scruffy couldn't jump on the bed and eat the fudge.

After he went to bed that night, Peter lay awake, listening. He smiled in the dark as he waited to hear what his mother said when she found her basket of fudge and her poem.

In his own house that night, Wishbone thought how happy Mrs. Dodge would be when she found the surprise. Then he made a valentine card for his mother, too, and left it on her pillow. He knew his mother wouldn't want fudge, even if he had some; she was always on a diet.

The next day, Peter said, "My mom liked her valentine. She said to tell you, thanks."

They delivered the two baskets to the people who had paid. Then Peter reached into his backpack. "Happy Valentine's Day," he said. He handed Wishbone two packages of Reese's Peanut Butter Cups. He'd had to get an advance on his allowance to buy them, but he didn't care. How many kids would have offered to give their fudge to Peter's mom? Not many, Peter thought.

Then he opened his blue notebook. "One good thing about us," he said, as he tore out the page titled *Sell Valentine Fudge* and crumpled it up. "We don't make the same mistake twice."

"That's right," said Wishbone. He unwrapped his candy and looked at all the pages remaining in the notebook. "We just make new mistakes."

Wishbone wondered what idea Peter would suggest next. A car wash? A lemonade stand? Whatever it was, Wishbone knew they would have fun doing it, whether they made any money or not.

"If at first you don't succeed," Peter said, as he turned the pages of his notebook.

"Cry, cry again," said Wishbone.

Hi, Tommy:

I haven't had time to make money
for my plane ticket because I went on
a camping trip with Wishbone and
his grandparents. We hiked and
fished. I learned to play Hearts and
his grandparents didn't care how late
we stayed up as long as we were
quiet. It was a blast.

Your friend,
Peter

7

Kathy for President

"We've decided to help you," Peter said. "Wishbone and I will be your publicity directors."

Kathy and Sharon did not look up. They were making posters that said, KATHY FOR PRESIDENT.

"With good publicity," Wishbone said, "you'll win for sure."

"We already have good publicity," Kathy said.

"Those posters?" Peter and Wishbone shook their heads.

"What's wrong with the posters?"

"Nothing's wrong with them," Peter said. "But if you want to be elected president of the Seventh-Grade Student Council, you need spots on the television news. Feature stories in the newspaper."

"Why not book me on the 'Today Show' while you're at it?" Kathy said.

"Maybe NBC could do a prime-time special," Sharon said.

The boys could tell from their sarcastic tone that the girls didn't think there was any chance of the newspapers or TV stations reporting a seventh-grade student council election.

"We got our picture in *The Herald* for the duck race," Wishbone said.

"All you need is an angle," Peter said. "A different slant that makes your story newsworthy."

"I've got it," Kathy said. "Nominee for Student Council President Murders Pesky Little Brother."

Peter and Wishbone looked at each other. It was a challenge.

"We will not only get a Kathy for President article in *The Herald*," Peter declared, "we will also get your campaign advertised on television."

Wishbone thought fast. "For a small fee," he added. "Good publicity directors don't work for free."

Peter gave him an approving look. He should have thought of that himself.

"If you get me on TV," said Kathy, "I'll give you all my worldly wealth."

"How much do you have?" Peter asked.

"Twenty dollars. But there's one condition. Don't bother me with every stupid idea. Just do what you're going to do and leave me alone."

"Agreed," said Peter.

"Agreed," said Wishbone.

Wishbone and Peter went outside and sat in their secret hiding place behind the lilac bush.

"How are we going to do it?" Wishbone said.

"An angle," Peter said. "We have to think of an angle."

That night, Peter paid careful attention to the six o'clock news. One man was interviewed because he was suing his church. There was a story about pollution in a local stream. Another segment showed people with picket signs on the steps of the state capitol.

Peter called Wishbone. "Let's picket," Peter said. "People with picket signs always get on the news."

"Who would we picket?" Wishbone asked.

"The mayor's office. Kathy will be on the news and we'll have a twenty-dollar profit."

"What does Mayor Finner have to do with the seventh-grade council? It isn't her fault if the students don't like school."

"That," said Peter, "is our angle. We won't picket because we don't like something, the way most pickets do. We'll picket to show that we're happy."

"Peter the Third," said Wishbone, "you are truly amazing." Then he added, "I think you have the *right* angle."

The next day, the two boys made picket signs:

WE LOVE OUR SCHOOL!!
FRANKLIN IS A GREAT TOWN
WE SAY NO TO DRUGS AND YES TO SCHOOL
WE DROOL OVER SCHOOL
MAYOR FINNER IS A WINNER

Each sign had a second, smaller line: Kathy Dodge for Seventh-Grade Council President.

Ten other kids agreed to carry a sign and march in front of the mayor's office at nine o'clock Saturday morning. Most of them did it because Peter and Wishbone assured them that a television news crew would be there, filming the pickets. Everyone thought it would be fun to be on TV.

"You are wasting your time," Annabelle said. "No TV station is going to film a bunch of kids with signs." She snickered. "Or did you get so rich already that you bought the TV station?"

Peter took a deep breath, the way his mother always did when she was angry, and wondered how much trouble he'd be in if he popped Annabelle a good one, right in the mouth. Too much, he decided as he let his breath out. Annabelle wasn't worth it.

"You're just jealous," Wishbone said, "because we're going to be on TV and you aren't."

Wishbone slept at Peter's house Friday night. At 8:30 Saturday morning, Peter called the local TV station and said, "Did you know that a group of students is planning to picket the mayor's office in half an hour?" Next he called *The Herald*.

"Let's hope it's a slow day for news," Wishbone said. "If there aren't any bank robberies or fires, maybe the station will follow up on your tip."

Kathy was still asleep when Peter and Wishbone left, lugging a stack of picket signs.

When they got to City Hall, they were surprised to see the parking lot full of cars. "The city offices are supposed to be closed on Saturday," Wishbone said.

A man walked past them, toward City Hall. "What's going on here today?" asked Peter.

"It's the mayors' convention. All the mayors in the state are here."

Peter grinned. "No candidate could ask for better publicity directors," he said.

Wishbone gave him a high five.

As soon as the other kids arrived, Peter and Wishbone handed out the signs and they all marched back and forth in front of City Hall. Within minutes, a group of people came out of City Hall. They stood on the steps and watched the pickets. Peter recognized Mayor Finner. She kept smiling and pointing at the signs.

A van pulled into the parking lot. On the side of the van, it said KFRN-TV.

"They came," Wishbone said.

Peter and Wishbone waited until the camera crew was out of the van. Then they climbed the steps of City Hall and stood beside Mayor Finner.

"On behalf of the Kathy Dodge for President committee," Peter said loudly, "we want to thank Mayor Finner for helping make Franklin such a great place to go to school."

The other kids cheered wildly and waved their picket signs in the air. Mayor Finner shook hands with Peter and Wishbone and thanked them for coming. Then she gave a brief speech, telling the people of Franklin that they have fine children. The camera recorded everything.

"Which one of you is Kathy?" one of the TV people asked.

"She isn't here," Peter said. "She's home."

"Do you know the address?"

Peter gave it. The TV crew piled back in the van and took off.

"We did it!" said Wishbone. "We got Kathy's campaign signs on television."

All the kids hurried home to be sure they didn't miss the noon news on KFRN.

When Peter and Wishbone got back to Peter's house, Kathy was fuming. "You flea brains!" she said. "Why didn't you tell me you were going to picket the mayors' convention? I got awakened out of a sound sleep by a TV crew pounding on the door, all excited about my campaign, and I didn't have a clue what they were talking about. I felt like an idiot."

"You told us not to bug you," Peter said. "You said you didn't want to know what we were going to do."

"If they show that interview on TV," Kathy said, "I will never go out in public again. I didn't even have time to comb my hair." She put both hands to her head and groaned. "I was wearing my Minnie Mouse pajamas."

The story was on the noon news. It showed the picketers. It showed Peter and Wishbone talking to Mayor Finner. And it showed Kathy, wearing Minnie Mouse pajamas, with her hair all tangled, saying, "My publicity directors are responsible for everything."

The reporter replied, "In addition to being a brilliant strategist, it appears this candidate is modest, too. We wish her luck in her campaign." The story ended with a close-up of a picket sign: Kathy Dodge for Seventh-Grade Council President.

"Every boy in the Franklin Middle School has now seen me in my Minnie Mouse pajamas," Kathy said. "I'm going to drop out of school and go live in the woods and eat berries."

The phone rang. Sharon cried, "You were on TV!"

"With my sheepdog hairdo," Kathy said. "I hoped no one was watching."

"You were great! You'll win the election for sure."

"You think anyone will vote for a person wearing Minnie Mouse pajamas? I looked like a nursery school reject."

"I didn't notice the pajamas," Sharon said.

The story ran again on the six o'clock news. This time, Mrs. Dodge taped it. There was an article about the pickets in *The Herald*, too. The Dodges' phone rang all evening. Kathy's friends called to congratulate her. Three kids that Kathy didn't know called to say they wanted to work on her campaign.

"You'll win by a landslide," Sharon predicted.

"You owe us twenty dollars," Peter said. At last he could repay Wishbone for the money Wishbone had lost on Peter's other ideas.

"I don't have twenty dollars," Kathy said.

"You promised! You said, if Wishbone and I got you on TV, you'd give us all your worldly wealth."

"And here it is," Kathy said. She dropped three coins into Peter's hand.

"Forty cents? What happend to the rest of it?"

"I bought new pajamas this afternoon. Sophisticated ones. If my publicity directors get me another interview, I want to be ready."

Tommy!

Big news!! Kathy got elected president of the Seventh-Grade Student
Council. I'll write and tell you all the
details when I have more time.

P.

8

The Liar's Contest

"Hey, Peter!" Annabelle hollered across the school playground. "Hey, Wishbone!"

Peter quit dribbling his basketball and watched Annabelle approach.

"Do you want to enter my Liar's Contest?" Annabelle said.

"What liar's contest?" Wishbone said.

"Each person tells a story that's mostly true but has one lie in it. The others have to say which part is the lie. It costs fifty cents to enter and there's a fabulous prize."

"How do you know who wins?" said Peter.

"The storyteller gets one point for each person who thinks his lie is true. If you correctly guess someone else's lie, you get one point. We add up all the points and the one with the most gets the prize."

"You mean," said Wishbone, "I might say I am Wishbone Wyoming and I'm nine years old and I have six sisters and a cat named Einstein. Then the others try to guess which statement is the lie."

"Exactly. I would say you don't really have a cat named Einstein."

"I win!" yelled Wishbone. "I DO have a cat named Einstein. But I don't have six sisters. I don't have any sisters."

"Then you'd get a point from me," Annabelle said. "But if you didn't have a cat named Einstein, I'd get the point from you. See how easy it is?"

Peter thought the contest sounded like fun but he wished someone other than Annabelle was running it. "What's the fabulous prize?" he asked.

"Money."

"How much money?"

"That," said Annabelle, "is a secret." She said the word *secret* mysteriously, as if it were a huge amount.

"Ha!" said Wishbone. "It will probably be one cent."

"You're the ones who want to get rich," Annabelle said. "Here's your chance."

"We'll think about it," Peter said, as he started dribbling the basketball again.

"The Liar's Contest is tomorrow after school," Annabelle said, "and the prize is terrific."

As soon as Annabelle left, Wishbone said, "What do you think? Should we do it?"

"I don't trust Annabelle. The contest is some kind of trick."

"She couldn't cheat. If everyone hears the stories at the same time, we'd all have an equal chance to get points. And Annabelle can afford to give a lot of prize money. If you win, it would be a good start on your plane ticket."

"If you win, you could get your DC-3 model kit."

"We're both good at telling stories," Peter said.

"It would be fun," Wishbone said.

"Let's do it," they said together.

That night, Kathy answered the phone, as usual, and then said, "It's for you, Peter. It's Wishbone *again*." She stressed *again* as if Wishbone's calls were a nuisance but Peter ignored her. No matter how often Wishbone called, Peter was always glad to talk to him.

"If one of us wins, let's split the money, fifty-fifty," Wishbone said.

"Agreed."

The next day after school, five kids paid Annabelle the entry fee for the Liar's Contest. They sat in a circle on the grass.

"Be alert," Peter whispered to Wishbone. "We'll have to think fast if we expect to know what's true and what isn't."

Mark was the first contestant. "When I was two years old," he said, "my family had a pet parakeet. One day I opened the cage and let Charlie out. I didn't know a window was open and he flew out and disappeared."

Mark talked faster and faster, as if he would forget the end of the story before he got to it. "My parents put an ad in the newspaper and told all the neighbors to watch for Charlie. Two weeks later, we got a telephone call from the manager of Burger King. Charlie was hanging around the parking lot, eating crumbs from hamburger buns. When we went over there, he came right to me."

Mark stopped and smiled. "Which part was the lie?" he said.

"The bird's name wasn't Charlie," said Wishbone.

"One point for me," said Mark.

"It wasn't Burger King," said Clinton. "It was McDonald's."

"One point for me," said Mark.

Susie and Annabelle guessed wrong, too.

Peter guessed last. "You weren't two years old," he said. "You were older."

Mark quit smiling. "How did you know?" he said.

"One point for me," said Peter.

The next person was Clinton. "My father," he

said, "saw a bank robbery and he yelled for the police. The robber shot at my father but he missed and the police caught the robber and my father got a five thousand dollar reward."

Peter had to guess first this time. "I think everything's true except it wasn't your father. It was someone else."

"That's right," said Susie. "That's what I was going to guess." Everyone else said they wanted to guess the same as Peter and Susie.

"That isn't fair," Clinton said. "I don't get any points."

"The story of that robbery was on the TV news last night," Wishbone said.

"I saw it, too," said Mark, "and it wasn't your father."

Susie's story stumped everyone; she got five points.

When it was Annabelle's turn, Peter listened carefully. If she tried anything tricky in her story, he wanted to catch it.

To his surprise, Annabelle's story wasn't believable at all. "When I was born," she said, "I was a Siamese twin. I had an operation when I was six weeks old to separate me from my twin. Unfortunately, the twin died. Otherwise, there would be another girl just like me."

Wishbone nudged Peter and rolled his eyes. Peter

knew exactly what Wishbone was thinking. They waited for Annabelle to continue but that was the end of her story.

It was Wishbone's turn to guess first. "Your whole story is a lie," he said, "all except the fact that you were born. You never had a twin."

Everyone else agreed. Annabelle said, "Oh, rats. I didn't think you'd know."

Peter squinted at her suspiciously. She didn't sound surprised, or unhappy. He had the uneasy feeling that she had known they would not believe she'd been a Siamese twin. But why would she purposely lose the contest? Didn't she want to keep the fabulous prize?

He had no time to wonder about it; it was his turn to tell a story. "Before I moved here," he said, "I lived in a yellow house that had a big maple tree in the yard. I fell out of the tree once and broke my leg and had to wear a cast. It snowed while I had the cast on, so I put a plastic bag over the cast and went sledding with my friends."

Everyone except Clinton guessed that Peter didn't really go sledding with a broken leg. Clinton guessed it was a broken arm, not a broken leg.

"You're all wrong," Peter said. "Everything I said is true except my house was white."

"Your mother's a nurse," said Wishbone. "She

wouldn't let you go sledding with a cast on your leg."

"She wasn't home," said Peter.

"It's time to add up the points," said Annabelle, after Wishbone had his turn. Everyone watched, to be sure she did it right.

Annabelle called out the scores. "Clinton: two points. Mark: three points. Annabelle: four points. Wishbone: seven points. Susie: eight points. Peter: nine points."

"I won!" cried Peter. "Where's my prize money?"

Annabelle said, "There isn't any prize money."

"You said the winner got a fabulous prize. You said it would be money."

"I lied."

They all stared at Annabelle.

"You knew this was a Liar's Contest," Annabelle said. "My lie was the best of all." And she walked away.

"She got all the entry fees and she didn't give any prize," Peter said.

"Cheater!" said Mark.

"I'm never going to talk to her again," said Susie.

"I knew we shouldn't trust her," said Peter.

"It was fun to make up stories, though," Wishbone said.

"And to guess which parts were true," added Mark.

"I think we should do it again some time," said Susie.

"Me, too," said Clinton. "My story would be better next time."

"Let's have a Liar's Club," said Peter. "We'll meet once a week and everyone will tell a story and we'll try to guess which part is true, just like we did today."

"Only there won't be any fifty-cent fee," said Wishbone.

"And there won't be any Annabelle," said Susie.

Everyone agreed to meet again in one week.

As Peter and Wishbone walked home, Peter kicked at a pebble. "Annabelle stinks," he said. "Why did she have to win?" He kicked the pebble again.

Wishbone said, "Annabelle didn't win. She lost."

"She has our money, doesn't she?"

"Annabelle got $2.50 in entry fees but everyone is mad at her. We got a fun new club with our friends. The way I see it, she's the loser." Wishbone took a chocolate bar out of his jacket pocket, unwrapped it, and offered half to Peter.

Peter took a bite. Wishbone always made him feel better. And the Liar's Club would be fun. Next time he wrote to Tommy, he would tell him about it. Maybe Tommy and Jason would want to have a Liar's Club, too.

Thinking about Tommy made him realize that he had not written to Tommy for several weeks. In fact, he had not even thought about Tommy for days and days. He hoped Tommy wasn't too lonely.

"You're right about one thing," Wishbone said. "Annabelle stinks."

Dear Tommy:

Sorry I haven't written but then, neither have you. I'm in a new club called The Liar's Club. The other members are all professional baseball players. Ha. Ha.

Your friend,
Peter

9

The Saturday Morning Lawn Service

"We are going to quit working so hard," Peter said.

"Good," answered Wishbone, as he bit one end off a Twinkie.

"Instead of working hard, we'll work smart."

Wishbone ate the other end.

Peter said, "The Saturday Morning Lawn Service is now open for business."

"Lawn Service! You think lawn mowing is easy?"

"We won't mow the lawns. We'll be the middlemen."

Wishbone ate the center of the Twinkie and waited.

"We get jobs to mow lawns," Peter said. "We charge five dollars per lawn. Then we hire other kids to do the work, and we pay them four dollars per lawn."

"We make a dollar on every job?"

Peter nodded. "And our hands never touch the lawn mowers."

"Won't the other kids get mad if they find out we're charging five dollars but only giving them four dollars?"

"That's our fee, for finding them the job. It's how all employment services work."

Wishbone nibbled the top off the second Twinkie. Then he tried to scoop out all the filling with his tongue.

"I already have one customer," Peter said. "Mrs. Harper wants her lawn mowed every week. She paid me in advance for one month." He showed Wishbone the twenty-dollar bill.

"Maybe Mark would like a job mowing Mrs. Harper's lawn," Wishbone said. "For sixteen dollars a month."

Mark did.

Peter and Wishbone went door to door, offering their Saturday Morning Lawn Service. Four other neighbors signed up.

"Now all we have to do is recruit the workers," Peter said.

Annabelle said her father hired a gardener, who not only mowed the grass but also planted flowers. Peter didn't ask Annabelle if she wanted one of the jobs.

Susie wanted money for a new album; she agreed to do one lawn. Three boys from the fifth-grade Little League team took the other three jobs.

Peter wrote everything in his blue notebook:

LAWN SERVICE

Customer	Worker	Time
Mrs. Harper	Mark	9 A.M.
Mr. & Mrs. Bither	Susie	10
Mrs. Lawrence	Eddie	Any time
Mrs. Neu	Herman	11
Mr. Klawson	Bobby	10 or later

Peter did some figuring. "We'll earn twenty dollars a month," he said. "Ten dollars each. This time, you'll get your DC-3."

"Let's get one more customer and I'll mow the lawn myself," Wishbone said. "The DC-3 model is expensive."

"What about your grandparents?"

Wishbone made a phone call. He told Grandpa Wyoming about the lawn service and added, "We're a cut above the others." When he hung up, he was laughing. "Grandpa says he hopes our business keeps growing."

Peter added to his list:

| Customer | Worker | Time |

Wishbone's grandparents Wishbone Any time

On Friday, Peter and Wishbone reminded all of their workers that they were supposed to mow a lawn the next morning. Everyone promised to remember.

Peter went to the fifth-grade Little League game Friday night but it was rained out. It was rescheduled for Saturday morning.

"This means I can't mow that lady's lawn," Eddie said. "I'm supposed to pitch."

"I'm starting at first base," Herman said.

"My dad's coming to the game, to watch me play," Bobby said. "I could mow for Mr. Klawson on Sunday instead."

"But I promised everyone we'd mow on Saturday morning."

Three voices said, "Sorry."

When Peter got home, Kathy said, "Mark called. He said to tell you he has to go somewhere with his parents and won't be able to mow Mrs. Harper's lawn."

Peter groaned and got out his notebook. Susie was the only worker who was going to do a lawn. He and Wishbone would be busy.

Peter dialed Wishbone's number. "He can't come to the phone," Mrs. Wyoming said. "He has a stomachache."

"Please ask him to call me in the morning," Peter said. "As early as possible. It's important."

The next morning, Wishbone's father called. "Wishbone is in the hospital," he said.

Peter sat down.

"He had his appendix removed last night," Mr. Wyoming said.

"Is he OK?"

"He had a hard night and he'll be sore for awhile, but he'll be fine in a few weeks. He asked me to call you. He's worried about your lawn service."

Not half as worried as I am, Peter thought, but he didn't say that. He said, "Tell him I'll take care of everything."

"You can tell him yourself, if you like," Mr. Wyoming said. "He can have visitors today between two and five."

Peter was at the Harpers' a few minutes before nine. It took almost an hour to cut their grass. Next he did Mr. Klawson's grass. As he pushed Mr. Klawson's lawn mower, he thought about Wishbone going to the hospital and having an operation. It scared him to think of Wishbone being so sick. He hoped Wishbone's stomach didn't hurt too much.

He got to Mrs. Lawrence's just after eleven. He hadn't noticed before how long her grass was. He had to stop every few minutes and empty the bag of clippings. When he finished, she gave him a turkey sandwich and a glass of milk. It felt good to sit down while he ate.

He was glad that The Saturday Morning Lawn Service had not expanded beyond his own neighborhood. At least he didn't have to walk far to get from one customer to the next. The muscles in Peter's legs ached.

It was one o'clock when he got to Mrs. Neu's house. Maybe he and Wishbone should change the name to The Saturday Lawn Service, instead of The Saturday Morning Lawn Service, in case this ever happened again.

Mrs. Neu had a power mower. "You look tired," she said, as she showed Peter how to work it. "Are you sure you can do this?"

"I'm sure," Peter said. He was determined to finish every job that The Saturday Morning Lawn Service had agreed to do. For once, his bright idea was not going to be a flop. He and Wishbone would have a profit.

When he was done, Mrs. Neu brought him a homemade cinnamon roll and a glass of apple juice. He lay on her grass for a few minutes after he ate. It was hard to get up again.

Wishbone's grandparents weren't home. Peter guessed they were probably at the hospital. He knew their lawn mower was in their garage and the side garage door was open.

He had never realized how big Wishbone's grandparents' yard was. Or how many trees there were to go around. Or how many slopes there were.

There were blisters between his thumb and forefinger on both hands, from pushing the mowers. His T-shirt stuck to his back; his neck ached. He was tempted to quit. Wishbone's grandparents would understand.

But then he thought about Wishbone; his partner in The Saturday Morning Lawn Service was in the hospital. He couldn't let his partner down.

At 2:45, he dragged the mower back in the garage and limped home.

"You look like you were in a dog fight and the dog won," Kathy said.

Peter stood in the shower and let the hot water pour over him. He shampooed his hair. He put on clean clothes. He counted the money he had earned. Everyone had paid him except Wishbone's grandparents; they still weren't home. Mrs. Neu and Mr. Klawson even gave him a tip.

It was 3:30. He had just enough time.

He got to the hospital fifteen minutes before visiting hours ended. The head of Wishbone's bed was elevated, so he was sitting up. His parents and grandparents were there. Wishbone looked pale but he smiled when he saw Peter.

Peter opened the bag he carried and handed Wishbone a gift-wrapped box. "This is to help you get well," he said.

Wishbone said, "I recognize the paper. Shetland's Toy Store." He unwrapped the package and let out a whoop. "It's my DC-3! It's the model I want! Oh, boy! This is terrific! This is . . ." He stopped yelling and looked at Peter. "This cost twenty-one dollars," he said. "Where did you get twenty-one dollars?"

"I spent the money from The Saturday Morning Lawn Service." He told Wishbone what had happened.

"You mowed ALL the lawns yourself?" Grandpa Wyoming said.

"All except the Bithers. Susie did theirs."

"It's a wonder they didn't have to bring *you* to the emergency room," Mrs. Wyoming said. "Imagine mowing five lawns in one morning."

"You finally made a profit," Wishbone said.

Peter nodded.

Wishbone looked at the DC-3. He looked at Peter. "You'll never save enough for a plane ticket if you spend your money as fast as you get it," he said.

"Some things are more important than money."

Wishbone said softly, "Thanks."

"Well, Winston," said Grandpa Wyoming. "You certainly have a generous friend."

Wishbone smiled at Peter for a long moment. "He's the best friend I ever had," he said.

Peter forgot all about his aching back and his blistered hands. The person he would have chosen at a Best Friend store, out of all the kids in town, had chosen him, too.

He reached into the bag again. "While I was cutting all that grass," he said, "I had lots of time to think and I had a great idea." He took out his blue notebook. "Let's have a poetry contest."

Wishbone said, "I've heard that *rhyme* doesn't pay."

Laughing, Peter opened the notebook. "We'll charge a 'handling fee' of one dollar per poem." As Peter turned to the page marked Poetry Contest, he knew he didn't care if he ever made $235. He had started out to raise money to leave town but now he wanted to stay. He would have a great summer vacation right here, with Wishbone.

"We need a list of rules," Wishbone said. He leaned over the side of the hospital bed, reaching for the notebook. He wrote, *Rule Number One: Poems must be no longer than one page.*

"It won't be easy to judge a poetry contest," Mrs. Wyoming said.

"We like a challenge," said Wishbone. "Right, partner?"

"Right," said Peter. "Besides, how else can we get rich quick?"

Dear Tommy:

I won't be coming this summer,
after all. I hope you are not too disappointed. Here are two entry blanks
for a poetry contest, in case you and
Jason need something to do until you
go to camp.
Wishbone and I are building a
DC-3 model together. I probably won't
have time to write much during vaca-
tion, because as soon as school is out,
Wishbone and I are going to open a
car wash and give our profits to The
Kettle Kitchen.

Your friend,
Peter Dodge, III

About the Author

Peg Kehret's popular novels for young people are regularly nominated for state awards. She has received the Young Hoosier Award, the Golden Sower Award, the Iowa Children's Choice Award, the Sequoyah Award, the Celebrate Literacy Award, the Pacific Northwest Young Reader's Choice Award, the Maud Hart Lovelace Award, and the New Mexico Land of Enchantment Award. She lives with her husband, Carl, and their animal friends in Washington State, where she is a volunteer at the Humane Society and SPCA. Her two grown children and four grandchildren live in Washington, too.

Peg's Minstrel titles included *Nightmare Mountain; Sisters, Long Ago; Cages; Night of Fear; Terror at the Zoo; Horror at the Haunted House;* and the *Frightmares*™ series.

TM

Whenever pets–and their owners–get into trouble, Rosie Saunders and Kayo Benton always seem to be in the middle of the action. Ever since they started the Care Club ("We Care About Animals"), they've discovered a world of mysteries and surprises. . .and danger!

#1: CAT BURGLAR ON THE PROWL 89187-1/$3.50

#2: BONE BREATH AND THE VANDAL 89189-8/$3.50

#3: DON'T GO NEAR MRS. TALLIE 89191-X/$3.99

#4: DESERT DANGER 89193-6/$3.99

#5: THE GHOST FOLLOWED US HOME 53522-6/$3.99

#6: RACE TO DISASTER 53524-2/$3.99

#7: SCREAMING EAGLES 53526-9/$3.99

#8: BACKSTAGE FRIGHT 53528-5/$3.99

By Peg Kehret

A MINSTREL® BOOK
Published by Pocket Books

Simon & Schuster Mail Order Dept. BWB
200 Old Tappan Rd., Old Tappan, N.J. 07675

Please send me the books I have checked above. I am enclosing $_____(please add $0.75 to cover the postage and handling for each order. Please add appropriate sales tax). Send check or money order--no cash or C.O.D.'s please. Allow up to six weeks for delivery. For purchase over $10.00 you may use VISA: card number, expiration date and customer signature must be included.

Name _____

Address _____

City _____ State/Zip _____

VISA Card # _____ Exp.Date _____

Signature _____ 1049-08

R·L·STINE'S
GHOSTS OF FEAR STREET ®

1 HIDE AND SHRIEK   52941-2/$3.99
2 WHO'S BEEN SLEEPING IN MY GRAVE?   52942-0/$3.99
3 THE ATTACK OF THE AQUA APES   52943-9/$3.99
4 NIGHTMARE IN 3-D   52944-7/$3.99
5 STAY AWAY FROM THE TREE HOUSE   52945-5/$3.99
6 EYE OF THE FORTUNETELLER   52946-3/$3.99
7 FRIGHT KNIGHT   52947-1/$3.99
8 THE OOZE   52948-X/$3.99
9 REVENGE OF THE SHADOW PEOPLE   52949-8/$3.99
10 THE BUGMAN LIVES!   52950-1/$3.99
11 THE BOY WHO ATE FEAR STREET   00183-3/$3.99
12 NIGHT OF THE WERECAT   00184-1/$3.99
13 HOW TO BE A VAMPIRE   00185-X/$3.99
14 BODY SWITCHERS FROM OUTER SPACE   00186-8/$3.99
15 FRIGHT CHRISTMAS   00187-6/$3.99
16 DON'T EVER GET SICK AT GRANNY'S   00188-4/$3.99
17 HOUSE OF A THOUSAND SCREAMS   00190-6/$3.99
18 CAMP FEAR GHOULS   00191-4/$3.99
19 THREE EVIL WISHES   00189-2/$3.99
20 SPELL OF THE SCREAMING JOKERS   00192-2/$3.99
21 THE CREATURE FROM CLUB LAGOONA   00850-1/$3.99
22 FIELD OF SCREAMS   00851-X/$3.99
23 WHY I'M NOT AFRAID OF GHOSTS   00852-8/$3.99
24 MONSTER DOG   00853-6/$3.99
25 HALLOWEEN BUGS ME   00854-4/$3.99
26 GO YOUR TOMB -- RIGHT NOW!   00855-2/$3.99
27 PARENTS FROM THE 13TH DIMENSION   00857-9/$3.99

HAPPY HAUNTINGS: COLLECTOR'S EDITION (contains Who's Been Sleeping in My Grave?,
Stay Away From the Tree House and Fright Knight)   02292-X/$6.99

Available from Minstrel® Books
Published by Pocket Books

Simon & Schuster Mail Order Dept. BWB
200 Old Tappan Rd., Old Tappan, N.J. 07675

POCKET
B O O K S

Please send me the books I have checked above. I am enclosing $_____(please add $0.75 to cover the
postage and handling for each order. Please add appropriate sales tax). Send check or money order--no cash
or C.O.D.'s please. Allow up to six weeks for delivery. For purchase over $10.00 you may use VISA: card
number, expiration date and customer signature must be included.

Name _____
Address _____
City _____ State/Zip _____
VISA Card # _____ Exp.Date _____
Signature _____ 1146-26

SPOOKSVILLE™

❏ **#1 The Secret Path** 53725-3/$3.50
❏ **#2 The Howling Ghost** 53726-1/$3.50
❏ **#3 The Haunted Cave** 53727-X/$3.50
❏ **#4 Aliens in the Sky** 53728-8/$3.99
❏ **#5 The Cold People** 55064-0/$3.99
❏ **#6 The Witch's Revenge** 55065-9/$3.99
❏ **#7 The Dark Corner** 55066-7/$3.99
❏ **#8 The Little People** 55067-5/$3.99
❏ **#9 The Wishing Stone** 55068-3/$3.99
❏ **#10 The Wicked Cat** 55069-1/$3.99
❏ **#11 The Deadly Past** 55072-1/$3.99
❏ **#12 The Hidden Beast** 55073-X/$3.99
❏ **#13 The Creature in the Teacher** 00261-9/$3.99
❏ **#14 The Evil House** 00262-7/$3.99
❏ **#15 Invasion of the No-ones** 00263-5/$3.99
❏ **#16 Time Terror** 00264-3/$3.99
❏ **#17 The Thing in the Closet** 00265-1/$3.99
❏ **#18 Attack of the Killer Crabs** 00266-8/$3.99
❏ **#19 Night of the Vampire** 00267-8/$3.99
❏ **#20 The Dangerous Quest** 00268-6/$3.99
❏ **#21 The Living Dead** 00269-4/$3.99
❏ **#22 The Creepy Creature** 00270-8/$3.99

BY CHRISTOPHER PIKE

Available from Minstrel® Books
Published by Pocket Books

Simon & Schuster Mail Order Dept. BWB
200 Old Tappan Rd., Old Tappan, N.J. 07675

Please send me the books I have checked above. I am enclosing $_____(please add $0.75 to cover the
postage and handling for each order. Please add appropriate sales tax). Send check or money order--no cash or C.O.D.'s
please. Allow up to six weeks for delivery. For purchases over $10.00 you may use VISA: card number, expiration date and
customer signature must be included.

Name _____

Address _____

City _____ State/Zip _____

VISA Card # _____ Exp.Date _____

Signature _____ 1145-20